*Quiet!*

Text copyright © 2018 Céline Claire
Illustrations copyright © 2018 Magali Le Huche
First edition copyright © 2018 Comme des géants inc.

Translation by Mireille Messier
Editorial and art direction by Nadine Robert
Book design by Jolin Masson

The illustrations in this book were made with ink and digitally colored.

This edition published in 2021 by Milky Way Picture Books,
an imprint of Comme des géants inc. Varennes, Quebec, Canada.

**Library and Archives Canada Cataloguing in Publication**

Title: Quiet! / Céline Claire ; illustrations, Magali Le Huche ; translation,
Mireille Messier. Other titles: Silence! English
Names: Claire, Céline, author.| Le Huche, Magali, 1979-illustrator. |
Messier, Mireille, 1971-translator.
Identifiers: Canadiana 20210042427 | ISBN 9781990252044 (hardcover)
Classification: LCC PZ7.1.C537 Qu 2021 | DDC j843/.92—dc23

ISBN: 978-1-990252-04-4

Printed and bound in China

**Milky Way Picture Books**
38 Sainte-Anne Street
Varennes, QC J3X 1R5
Canada

www.milkywaypicturebooks.com

# Quiet!

Story by
Céline Claire

Art by
Magali Le Huche

Milky Way
Picture Books

Mister Martin liked peace and quiet.

Drinking his coffee in silence…

reading his newspaper quietly…

taking a nap in peace.

Yes, what Mister Martin liked most of all was…

# QUIET!

His neighbors knew this, so they tried
to do everything quietly.

They were very careful for the first five minutes…

then, they were a little bit less careful...

and then even less so…

until they wound up forgetting that what
Mister Martin liked most of all was…

# QUIET!

Mister Martin was fed up
with his neighbors' ruckus.
He went to find a solution.

"I can't stand it anymore!
There's too much noise when I'm drinking my coffee,
too much commotion when I'm eating my soup.
And at night… Aaah! At night…"

The clerk thought for a moment.

"You want silence? Lots and lots of silence?
Here is something that will change your life!"

Mister Martin looked at the price and thought
it was a bit expensive. But silence is golden,
so he paid and took the magic product home.

"Pour the magic product into
the tub and add 150 liters of water."

"Take a butterfly net and remove the netting."

"Dip the frame of the net into the tub.
Then, pull it out...

and quickly go outside."

"Blow, and blow, and blow until you can blow no more."

"Step into the bubble and let it harden for three days and three nights (plug your ears, in the meantime, if necessary)."

"And listen to the silence."

Mister Martin listened,
but he couldn't hear a thing.
He closed his eyes and opened his ears,
but he couldn't hear a thing.
He opened the windows and the doors
of his home, but he couldn't hear a thing.

And so, in silence, he jumped for joy!

For the first time, Mister Martin
drank his coffee in silence, read his newspaper
quietly, and took his nap in peace.

And the next day, Mister Martin
drank his coffee in silence, read his newspaper
quietly, and took his nap in peace.

And the day after that, Mister Martin
drank his coffee in silence, read his newspaper
quietly, and took his nap in peace.

When he put his ear up to the bubble wall,
he couldn't hear a thing.

When he tapped
his finger on the bubble,
no one could hear
a thing, either.

The silence
was deafening.

Mister Martin wondered:
Could anyone see him?
Could anyone hear him?

The only answer was silence.

The world must have forgotten him.

He suddenly felt all alone.
In silence.

And time passed noiselessly.

Until one day, finally, a little boy heard
Mister Martin's silence speaking volumes.

People started making noise about Mister Martin being
walled up in silence. The neighbors rushed to his side.
"Mister Martin is suffering in silence!"
"We have to help him!"
"The silence must be broken!"

The mailman kicked the bubble,
but the wall was too thick.

The lion tamer made one last attempt, but to no avail.

Mister Martin remained a prisoner of silence.

So the children, whose voices were so clear
and bright, looked at one another.

They opened their mouths, filled their lungs,
set their vocal cords in motion and a sound came out…
small, soft, but not quite enough.

They let it build, grow louder, grow deeper, amplify,
so much so that the sphere vibrated and
split in a long zigzag that spread and widened…

and the bubble burst into twenty thousand pieces
with a tremendous BANG! And Mister Martin exploded with joy.

He had liked the sound so much,
that his neighbors were speechless.

Suddenly, a car honked.
A dog barked.

The children went
back to their games.

And Mister Martin started to dance,
and dance, and dance some more!

All of these noises made sweet music.

The sweet music of life.

# The End